I CANNOT GET OVER MY EX

KUSUMA RAFEEQ

Dedicated to my ex.

Contents

CHAPTER ONE

The Echo

The rain hit the windows like tiny fists, demanding to be let in. Aryan sat on the edge of the bed that once belonged to both of them, staring at the ghost of her smile etched into the photo frame. His fingers hovered over his phone for the seventh time that morning, and once again, he stopped himself. His thumb knew the motion by heart—search, tap, call—but his chest clenched each time. What would he say, anyway? What could he possibly say that would change the end?

He had deleted her number. But his memory had not. Her number was tattooed onto the corners of his mind like a cruel joke.

Every corner of the apartment whispered her name. The books she never finished, dog-eared at chapters she claimed she'd come back to. The tea mug she insisted on using, now chipped. The scent of vanilla and citrus in the blanket he refused to wash. Aryan had thought time would dull the sharpness of her absence, but instead, it honed it to a blade.

"You have to move on," his best friend Kabir had told him last night over beers and burnt pizza, the kind Maya used to fix in seconds with just a flick of her wrist and some oregano.

Aryan had only nodded. But in his chest, the truth bloomed quietly: I don't want to. Not because he believed she'd come back, but because letting go felt like letting a part of himself die.

He got up and opened his laptop. Writing helped sometimes. He opened a blank document and typed:

"I cannot get over my ex."

The cursor blinked. Judging. Waiting. Like everyone else.

The Day She Left

It wasn't loud. There were no slammed doors or raised voices. It was the silence that screamed the loudest.

She had packed lightly—just the essentials. The sound of the zipper haunted him now, crisp and final. Aryan remembered standing in the hallway, the smell of rain on her coat as she looked at him with eyes that held both apology and resignation.

"I can't do this anymore," Maya said. Her voice was even, calm. Almost rehearsed.

Aryan didn't ask her to stay. He stood frozen, shocked by the ordinariness of the moment. He had expected a storm, not a quiet surrender. Her final kiss wasn't even on the lips—it was on the cheek, like a memory already fading.

He replayed that moment in his head a hundred times. What if he had stopped her? What if he had cried, pleaded? But the questions always arrived too late, like the words he always wished he'd said.

And just like that, she was gone. No dramatic music. No thunder. Just a click of the door and a forever etched into silence.

CHAPTER THREE

Kabir's Rules of Getting Over Someone

Kabir had three rules:

- Delete their pictures.
- Block them on everything.
- Sleep with someone else.

Aryan had followed none.

Her photos still lived on his cloud drive, organized into folders by year, event, and mood. There was one from their first trip to Coorg—her nose red from the cold, her eyes squinting with laughter, arms wrapped around him like a promise. He couldn't bring himself to delete it. Not when it held the purest version of who they had been.

He never blocked her. He wanted to. He even opened the settings more than once. But what if she messaged? What if she missed him one day? That tiny hope was poisonous, and yet, it was the only thing that made breathing bearable some days.

And the third rule—Kabir's grand finale—felt like betrayal. The idea of touching someone else felt wrong, like painting over a masterpiece that had been torn. It wasn't about physicality. It was about the weight behind every glance, every brush of skin. Maya had touched him with intention, with understanding. Anything less now felt empty.

"You're being dramatic," Kabir said one evening. "You were together for what, two years? You'll find someone else."

Aryan didn't argue. He just sipped his beer and watched the condensation roll down the bottle like it too had something to mourn.

Because it wasn't about how long. It was about how deep.

Maya had seen him in ways no one else had. She'd known how he liked his coffee when he was sad—black, strong, no sugar. She could tell when he needed silence instead of advice. She knew the weight he carried behind his jokes.

You don't get over someone like that.

You learn to carry them differently.

CHAPTER FOUR

The Unsent Letters

Aryan started writing letters he never intended to send.

They began as short notes—unfinished thoughts typed in the Notes app at 2 AM. But soon they became longer, handwritten on old paper with corners curling from time and regret. There was something sacred about writing them down, like performing a ritual no one would ever witness.

"Dear Maya," one letter began. "I saw a woman on the train today with your hair. I nearly followed her to her stop. Isn't that insane?"

Another letter read, "I wish I could tell you how the world has kept spinning without you, but I haven't. Not really."

He wrote about their shared laughter over roadside chaat, about the song that always played when they took road trips. About the day she cried in his arms and said, "Don't ever let go," and how he foolishly believed that love, once spoken, was forever.

Writing became a way to speak into the void, hoping the echo would ease the ache. He stacked the letters in a wooden box she once gifted him for his journals. It still carried the faint scent of sandalwood, mixed now with the dust of days gone quiet.

One evening, Aryan sat in front of a fire pit with Kabir, the box of letters beside him. He considered burning them. A symbolic release. But as the first flame licked the edge of one page, he pulled it back.

"Not yet," he whispered.

Some wounds need to bleed a little longer before they can scar.

CHAPTER FIVE

Her Birthday

He hadn't written the date down, but his body remembered. The ache in his chest that morning wasn't ordinary.

It was Maya's birthday.

He got up earlier than usual. Made coffee—black, no sugar, just the way she liked it. He let the bitterness rest on his tongue longer than necessary. Each sip a prayer, a memory.

He wandered into the market, aimless at first. Until he found himself in front of her favorite flower stall. The marigolds were bright, unapologetically alive. Just like her. The florist didn't recognize him, but Aryan remembered the day Maya had danced here, a flower tucked behind her ear, asking strangers to smile. He bought a bouquet.

Then he walked to the park near the university. The bench where they used to sit, watching kids run by, dreaming of futures that would now never arrive. He placed the marigolds on the bench and sat beside them.

He imagined her sitting beside him. Her laughter. The way she'd pull him into conversation with strangers. The way she'd hold his hand like it anchored her to this earth.

A little girl ran past, giggling, and Aryan felt something shift. Not a healing. But a moment of grace.

He didn't cry. Not then.

But later that night, he lit a candle beside the box of letters. Whispered a happy birthday into the quiet.

And for the first time in months, he let the silence answer him.

CHAPTER SIX

The Letters That Stayed

It had been a week since Maya's birthday. The marigolds had wilted on the park bench, but Aryan hadn't returned to see. He didn't need to. Some goodbyes are meant to stay said.

He sat now in his study, the same room where he'd once drafted stories for deadlines and dreamt of bestsellers. For months, his mind had been a static blur, creativity choked by grief. But something had shifted. Not a grand, cinematic moment of clarity—just a quiet settling, like dust finding its place.

The letters still filled the wooden box. He had written three more since Maya's birthday. But they were different now. Not aching with desperation, but filled with fragments of gratitude. Memories no longer written to keep her close, but to let her go—gently.

"Dear Maya," he wrote one evening, pen gliding smoother than it had in months, "I made your tea today. The one with cardamom and too much sugar. I hated it. But I smiled."

Another note: "I finally wrote something new today. Not about you. Not about us. It felt... okay. Like stretching after a long sleep."

The letters were no longer a cry into the void. They were quiet affirmations that he was still here. Still breathing. Still capable of feeling something other than loss.

Kabir noticed, too.

"You look lighter," he said, tossing Aryan a beer during one of their Friday catch-ups. "Still tragic as hell, but less like a haunted poet."

Aryan laughed—a real one this time. "I think I'm learning to carry her differently."

Kabir nodded. "Good. Because I was about to stage an intervention with puppies and sad indie music."

Later that night, Aryan sat by the window as the rain began again, softer this time, like a lullaby. He opened a new document, not a letter this time, but the beginnings of a story. Fiction, maybe. Or something like it. About love, and loss, and the strange ways we survive each other.

He didn't know how it would end.

But for the first time, he wasn't afraid to find out.

CHAPTER SEVEN

The Stranger in the Mirror

Two months had passed since Maya's birthday.

Aryan sat at his desk, morning light slanting through the half-open blinds. The apartment was finally quiet—not in a haunted way, but in a peaceful way. The kind of quiet that doesn't scream. That waits, gently, for you to fill it.

His journal lay open. Today's entry wasn't a letter to Maya.

It was a letter to himself.

> *"Dear Aryan,*
> *You survived. Maybe not gracefully. Maybe not completely. But you did.*
> *You're still here. And that counts."*

He paused, tapping the pen against his lips. Then continued:

> *"There will be days where it all rushes back.*
> *Where a laugh or a smell will take you back to her.*
> *Let it. But don't unpack your bags there.*
> *You're allowed to remember. Just don't forget*

yourself in the process."

He leaned back, rereading the words. They didn't sting. They didn't sing either. But they sat with him like an old friend who knew when to speak, and when not to.

Later that afternoon, Aryan shaved. Properly. Not the lazy stubble-trim he'd resorted to in the haze of grief, but a full, clean shave. He wore the indigo shirt Maya had gifted him two birthdays ago. It still fit, though it clung to him differently—tighter in the chest, looser in the sleeves. He had changed. Inside and out.

He stood before the mirror again. This time not searching for sadness, but for someone he could learn to recognize again.

He looked into his own eyes and said out loud, "You're going to be okay."

It didn't feel like a lie.

That evening, Kabir called. "There's a book launch downtown. Small crowd. Poetry. Free wine. You in?"

Aryan almost said no. That familiar ache tried to pull him back into the comfort of sorrow. But then he remembered the letter from the morning. The promise he'd made to himself.

He grabbed his jacket. "Yeah," he said. "I think I am."

And for the first time in a long while, Aryan stepped out—not to forget her, but to remember himself.

CHAPTER EIGHT

The Shift

It wasn't dramatic.

There was no epiphany, no thunderclap moment where the skies cleared and the weight lifted. But one morning, Aryan woke up and realized he hadn't thought of Maya the second he opened his eyes.

It was the third thought.

Progress, maybe.

He didn't rush to his phone, didn't check her last seen or scroll through old pictures before brushing his teeth. Instead, he watered the small plant by the window—a wilting fern he had bought during a lonely afternoon. It was still alive. Barely. But it was something.

In a session with Ananya, he mentioned it. "I think I forgot her for a moment," he said, then quickly added, "Not really. But... maybe the edge is duller."

Ananya offered a quiet smile. "That's how healing often starts. In the moments you don't notice."

Aryan wasn't sure if he believed in healing yet. But he noticed he no longer reached for her mug. That he started reading a new book without picturing her dog-earing the pages. That he could listen to their song on the radio without skipping it halfway through.

Some memories still hurt. Some days still folded him into silence.

But there were other moments now. A joke from Kabir that actually made him laugh. A colleague noticing his cologne. A small child offering him a crayon in the metro.

Little things. Incomplete things.

But maybe that's how you begin again—not by forgetting, but by remembering a little less sharply.

The Unspoken Conversation

Aryan wasn't sure when it started, but there were days when he found himself thinking about Maya not as the woman he had lost, but as the person she had become.

It happened in moments of quiet, when he wasn't trying to fill the space with thoughts of their past. He would catch snippets of conversation in cafés, the sound of her laugh at the back of his mind, the vision of her wearing that old jacket she used to steal from him, just for warmth.

But now, these memories no longer felt as painful. They felt like an old photograph—something beautiful that existed in its own time. They weren't trying to define his present anymore.

One afternoon, Aryan found himself walking through the same street where they had once lived together. The neighborhood looked the same, but he had changed. He no longer looked over his shoulder, half-expecting to bump into her at the grocery store or see her at the local bookstore. He was learning to live without that sense of waiting.

It was then that he saw her.

Maya was sitting at a café, one of the old ones they used to frequent on lazy afternoons. Her back was turned, but Aryan recognized the curve of her shoulders, the way she leaned slightly forward, a quiet concentration in her posture.

For a split second, he wanted to turn around, leave without saying a word. But his feet betrayed him. They carried him toward her, step by step, like they had known all along that he would do this.

She didn't see him at first. He stood there, unsure. A lifetime of shared memories, of shared silence, hung between them like an invisible thread.

"Maya?" he said, his voice rough from disuse.

She turned, her eyes widening in surprise. For a moment, neither of them said anything. The air seemed to still around them, as if holding its breath.

"Aryan?" she whispered, like she wasn't sure he was real.

"Yeah," he said, the word feeling foreign in his mouth. "I didn't expect to see you here."

Maya smiled softly. It wasn't the smile he remembered, the one that could light up the whole room, but something gentler. Something older.

"I come here sometimes," she said. "It still feels like home."

Aryan nodded. "I get that. I come here too, now. Just to... remember, I guess."

Her smile faltered slightly, and Aryan could see a flicker of the old pain in her eyes. But it was fleeting, quickly replaced by a calm he hadn't expected.

They sat down at the table, the space between them filled with so many things that neither one of them dared to touch. The words they hadn't said, the goodbye that still lingered, the questions that had never been answered.

"I've been meaning to reach out," Maya said quietly, stirring her coffee, her gaze avoiding his. "But I didn't know what to say."

Aryan felt his chest tighten. Part of him wanted to say everything that had been eating at him, to ask her why she left, why she didn't try harder, why everything had fallen apart. But another part of him knew that the answers wouldn't make a difference.

"It's okay," he said instead, his voice softer than he had intended. "I understand. I didn't reach out either. I guess I didn't want to disturb the quiet."

Maya's eyes met his, and for the first time in what felt like forever, Aryan saw the woman he had once known. Not his ex, not the person he had tried so hard to forget, but Maya—the woman who had once been the center of his world.

"I've missed you," she said, her voice barely a whisper.

Aryan's heart skipped a beat, but he didn't respond right away. He didn't know how to.

"I've missed you too," he finally said, his words honest but heavy. "But I think I've missed someone else more. The person I was when we were together. I don't know if that makes sense."

Maya nodded slowly, her fingers tracing the rim of her cup. "It does. I think I understand. I've missed me too. The person I was when I was with you."

And just like that, everything felt simpler. It wasn't about trying to pick up the pieces of what had been broken. It wasn't about resurrecting something that had died. It was about accepting that they were two people who had once fit perfectly together, and now they were two people who had to fit into a different version of themselves.

Neither of them reached for the past in that moment. They just sat there, quietly understanding that some things had ended, and that it was okay to let them rest.

The conversation was brief, but in that brief moment, Aryan realized something important.

Letting go didn't mean forgetting. It meant honoring what had been without trying to make it more than it was.

When he stood to leave, he didn't feel the familiar sting of loss. Instead, he felt a quiet peace. A sense of acceptance. Maya had been a part of his life, but she didn't need to be his entire life. Not anymore.

As he walked away, he glanced back once, but this time, he didn't need to see her to know she was there.

She was just a memory now. One that no longer had the power to break him.

CHAPTER TEN

The Space Between

Weeks passed, and Aryan found himself adjusting to the new rhythm of his life. The sharp edges of loss that had once ruled him, the kind of pain that made it hard to breathe or see straight, began to soften. It was still there, tucked away like a scar hidden beneath his skin, but it no longer dictated his every moment.

He didn't see Maya again. Their brief encounter had been a quiet closure, one that didn't need further words or explanations. It was enough to know that they had each stepped away from the past, from what could have been, and into the future, however uncertain it might seem.

But the space between them was not just a physical distance. It was a vast stretch of silence, of unspoken things, that neither of them dared to breach. They had both moved on, or at least were trying to, but the question lingered—what did it mean to move on from someone you had once loved with everything you had?

Aryan found himself asking that often. It wasn't about finding someone else, not right now. It wasn't about erasing Maya from his life, though it had once felt like that was the only way to survive. It was about learning how to exist in a world without the person who had once been the center of it all.

One evening, as Aryan sat in his apartment after another long day at work, his phone buzzed. It was an email—an old one, from Maya. His heart skipped, but there was no rush to open it. He had learned that sometimes, waiting was the hardest part of moving on. He read the subject line:

"I've been thinking about you."

It was a simple line. And yet, it carried so much weight. He stared at the screen for a long time before clicking open the email.

"Hey Aryan," it began, in the way only Maya could write—a mixture of warmth and hesitation. "I've been thinking about you a lot lately. I guess I never really thanked you for everything. For being with me when I needed it most, for loving me the way you did. I never really said goodbye properly, and maybe it's too late, but I wanted you to know that I'm grateful for all of it. I hope you're doing okay. I hope you're finding peace."

There was more, but Aryan didn't need to read the rest right away. He closed his eyes and took a deep breath. It wasn't a love letter, not really. It was a farewell, but one that was gentle, full of closure without expectation.

He had always believed that closure had to be a dramatic thing, something that needed to be said face to face, in words that were sharp and final. But Maya had given him something more profound—an understanding, a quiet acceptance of what had been, without the pressure of reawakening what had been left behind.

He typed a reply, though he hesitated at first. His fingers hovered over the keys, unsure of what he could say that would feel right.

"Thank you, Maya. For everything too. You were a huge part of my life, and I will never forget that. I don't know if I'm okay yet, but I'm getting there. I'm still learning, still figuring it out. But I think I'll be okay. I hope you are too."

He pressed send before he could second-guess himself.

The next few days were quiet. Aryan didn't dwell on Maya's email; he didn't let it consume him. It was just another moment, another piece of the puzzle of his life.

But in the weeks that followed, something strange happened. He began to notice the space between things. The spaces between thoughts, between moments of grief and healing, between the past and the present.

It wasn't an emptiness. It wasn't a void that begged to be filled. It was a space that allowed him to breathe, to reflect, to exist without the weight of expectation. It was the space where he could still miss Maya, but also begin to see the world again—not through the lens of loss, but through the possibility of new beginnings.

Aryan started going to the gym regularly. Not to escape, but to reconnect with his body, with his strength, with the person he had once been before everything became about loss. He signed up for a cooking class—a small step toward something new, something that didn't involve the ghosts of his past.

He began spending time with Kabir again, though their conversations had shifted. They no longer spoke about Maya or what had gone wrong. Instead, they talked about their work, about the future, about the things they could do and the lives they could build.

One evening, as Aryan sat on the balcony of his apartment, watching the city lights flicker below him, he realized that the space between things—the quiet, the waiting, the healing—wasn't something to fear.

It was something to embrace.

He had lived in the space for so long, waiting for the past to come back, for Maya to come back, for something to change. But now, he understood that the space itself was not an enemy. It was where growth happened. It was where new things were born.

And for the first time in a long time, Aryan felt something like hope stir in his chest.

CHAPTER ELEVEN

The Box

The box sat on the shelf, gathering dust in a corner of Aryan's apartment. He hadn't touched it in weeks. Maybe months. But it was there—always there—quietly watching over him like an old, forgotten relic of a life that had once been his.

It was a simple wooden box. Nothing extravagant. No intricate carvings or gilded edges. It had been a gift from Maya, on their first anniversary. She had given it to him with a smile, her eyes sparkling with that same playful warmth she always had when she made him something. He remembered how she had wrapped it in red paper, and how, despite the simplicity of the gift, it had felt like the most important thing in the world at that moment.

"I made this for you," she had said, her voice filled with such tenderness that it made his heart ache. "For all your thoughts. For everything you never say out loud."

Aryan had been speechless when he opened it. Inside, nestled carefully in the soft velvet lining, were small pieces of paper—scraps, really. Each one contained a memory, a feeling, a moment they had shared. Some were written in her neat handwriting, others were scrawled hastily when they had been in a rush, but each one was filled with a piece of their love, a piece of her soul. There were no grand gestures. Just words, simple and raw.

"There's more in there," Maya had smiled, nudging him gently, "for when you're missing me. When you don't know what to say, when you don't know how to feel... those are the days this will help."

Now, months later, Aryan sat on the floor, his fingers brushing the worn edges of the box, feeling the weight of it in his hands as though it had become a part of him. He had avoided it for so long, telling himself that the memories inside were too painful to revisit. But today, something was different. The ache in his chest was quieter now, but it was still there. It always would be, in some form. But the curiosity—no, the need to understand, to feel, to remember—was stronger than the pain.

He placed the box on his lap, his hands trembling slightly. The last time he had opened it had been before everything had ended. Before the silence had settled in. Before Maya had walked out the door, leaving a hole in his life that no one could fill. He hadn't opened it after that, convinced that revisiting those memories would only make the loss sharper, more unbearable.

But now, the silence was heavier than it had ever been. His mind had become an echo of the past, replaying their conversations, their laughter, the feel of her hands in his. It was a haunting kind of nostalgia. One that had lingered, refusing to let him go. He knew he wasn't going to find closure in this box. But maybe, just maybe, he could find the pieces of her that he had lost.

With a sigh, he slowly lifted the lid.

The first note was simple: "Do you remember the day we met?"

It was written in the elegant, looping handwriting that he had always admired. The words stirred something deep within him, and he found himself reading the note over and over. He remembered that day as if it were yesterday—the way her smile had been so effortless, the way her eyes had held a kind of mischief that made him feel both nervous and alive at the same time. She had walked into that café with a confidence that was magnetic, and he had been drawn to her immediately, like a moth to a flame.

"I think we were meant to meet that day," she had written. "There were a thousand things that could have kept us apart, but we found each other anyway."

A soft laugh escaped Aryan's lips as he closed his eyes, remembering the awkward way they had stumbled through their first conversation, both of them pretending to be cool, pretending to be unaffected by the undeniable chemistry between them.

The next note was more recent, one that Maya had written just a few months before everything had ended. The ink was faint, as if she had written it in a hurry, not realizing how much the words would weigh on her in the future.

"I'm scared, Aryan. I don't know if I can do this anymore."

Her words hit him like a physical blow. He had seen the fear in her eyes that day, heard it in her voice when they had talked about their future. But he hadn't understood it. He hadn't seen the signs, hadn't recognized the growing distance between them. How could he have? They were in love, weren't they? How could that ever change?

But Maya had felt it. The fear. The doubt. The cracks that had started to form in their foundation long before either of them had dared to admit it.

Tears welled in Aryan's eyes as he clutched the paper, feeling the weight of her confession. He had always thought that if he could just hold on, if he could just make her believe in them again, they could make it work. But Maya had known. She had seen it before he did.

The next note was a memory he had long forgotten—"The night we stayed up talking about our dreams until the sun came up." Aryan could see it so clearly now, how they had sat on the rooftop of her apartment, wrapped in blankets, with mugs of tea in hand. They had talked about everything—about where they wanted to go, what they wanted to become. Maya had talked about traveling the world, about painting, about finding herself in places she'd never been. Aryan had listened, mesmerized by the passion in her voice, by the way she saw the world as an endless canvas. He had shared his own dreams, his own quiet hopes, but as he read the note, he realized that somewhere along the way, they had stopped dreaming together. Their paths had diverged, and neither of them had known how to find their way back to each other.

He folded the note and placed it back in the box. His fingers shook as he reached for the next one.

It was a simple, unmarked piece of paper. There were no words on it, just the faint outline of her handwriting, as though she had started to write something but had stopped midway. The absence of words hit him harder than anything else. It was as if she had been too afraid to speak, too afraid to put into words the things that had been left unsaid between them.

The box was now empty. Aryan looked down at the small pile of memories, each note a fragment of what they had shared. He felt a sense of finality. Not a sense of closure—he knew that wasn't something he would ever find—but a sense of acceptance. The love they had shared was real. The moments they had experienced together were genuine. But sometimes, love wasn't enough to hold two people together. Sometimes, people outgrow each other, and no amount of nostalgia or memory could change that.

Aryan closed the box and placed it gently on the shelf. He didn't know if he would open it again, or if it would sit there, collecting dust, a reminder of a love that had been.

But for now, it was enough.

He had held onto it long enough to understand something important—that the memories didn't have to define him. They didn't have to be a weight around his neck. They could be a part of him, yes, but not the whole of him. He was more than the sum of his past.

And maybe, just maybe, that was enough to start moving forward.

CHAPTER TWELVE

Acceptance

It was quiet now. The kind of quiet that draped over everything like a heavy blanket, making it hard to breathe, hard to think. Aryan sat on the edge of the bed, the room dimly lit by the soft, golden glow of the lamp. His fingers trembled slightly as he held the cup of tea, but he couldn't bring himself to drink it. The warmth seeped into his skin, but it didn't reach the coldness lodged deep inside his chest.

He had spent so many months tangled in the wreckage of their love, trying to fix what was broken, trying to patch up the cracks that had formed between them. He had gone through all the motions—long nights of restless thoughts, desperate conversations with friends who had all said the same things, empty promises to himself that one day, he'd wake up and feel different. That one day, he'd wake up and be okay.

But he wasn't okay. Not yet. Maybe not ever.

Acceptance, he had learned, wasn't something that came in a flash. It didn't arrive like a light bulb turning on. It crept in slowly, like fog settling over a landscape, obscuring everything around you until you weren't sure where you were anymore. And yet, somehow, you learned to breathe through it. To exist in it. It was neither easy nor graceful. It was like learning to live with a wound that would never completely heal, a scar that would always remind you of what you had lost.

The photos were still there. The texts. The old playlists. He hadn't deleted them, not yet. They were remnants of something beautiful. Beautiful and broken. The weight of it all was suffocating, but there was a certain tenderness in the pain. He wasn't sure how else to explain it. The pain was a reminder of a time when he had been fully alive in her arms, when the world had felt right, when everything had made sense.

But that was over.

And today, for the first time in a long time, Aryan felt the shift. It was subtle. Like the turn of a page, or the way the light changes just before dawn. But it was there. A shift in his chest, a softening of the edges. Something inside him had cracked open, and for the first time, he was able to sit in the quiet of it and not feel desperate to fill the silence with answers.

He had been so consumed with the idea of fixing things. With trying to figure out where it had gone wrong. Trying to make sense of the pieces that no longer fit. He had blamed himself, blamed her, blamed time. But today, in the silence of his apartment, in the solitude of his own company, something finally clicked.

It wasn't about blame. It wasn't about fixing it. It wasn't about holding on to something that was never meant to last forever.

It was about learning to live without her. Learning to be okay with the absence. To let the grief breathe, without trying to chase it away. To allow himself to mourn, to cry, but also to smile. To forgive himself for the things he couldn't change, and to forgive her for the things she hadn't been able to give him.

His phone buzzed, a reminder of the world still turning outside his little bubble of grief. A message from Kabir: "I'm meeting someone tonight. Join me? I know you haven't been out in a while."

Aryan stared at the message, his thumb hovering over the keyboard as he debated whether to respond. For the first time in a long time, he didn't feel the familiar urge to retreat into himself. He didn't feel the intense need to stay inside, where everything was safe and quiet and painful, but familiar. He didn't have the energy to pretend everything was fine, but he also didn't want to let the world pass him by.

Okay, he typed. I'll be there.

And just like that, with a single action, Aryan allowed himself to step forward. Not into a new life, not yet. But into a life that wasn't defined by what he had lost. A life that was his, outside of the echo of Maya's absence.

The moment he pressed send, a weight lifted off his chest, and for the first time, he felt the lightness of it. Not the kind of lightness that came from pretending he wasn't hurting, but the kind that came from accepting the hurt as a part of him, as something that would always be there but no longer control him.

He put the cup of tea down, the warmth no longer something he needed to hold onto. He stood up, his legs unsteady at first, but then strong. For the first time in months, he was able to look at his reflection in the mirror without the familiar knot in his stomach. The man staring back at him was still the same. Still scarred. Still a little broken. But also, undeniably, still him.

"I'm sorry, Maya," he whispered to the empty room. The words felt different now, softer. Not an apology to fix things, not an apology that could change the past, but an apology that allowed him to release her, to release himself. "I'm sorry I couldn't be the person you needed me to be. But I'm trying now. I'm trying to be the person I need to be."

The tears came then—not the heavy sobs that had wracked his body in the early days of their breakup, but soft, quiet tears that fell down his face like rain, washing away the remnants of guilt and regret that had clung to him for so long.

He didn't know if he would ever fully "move on" from Maya. How could he? She had been the center of his world for so long. But he knew, with a strange clarity, that moving on wasn't the goal. Acceptance was.

And for the first time, Aryan was beginning to understand that true acceptance didn't mean letting go of love. It meant letting love live in a different way—without pain, without expectation. A love that could exist in memories, in moments that had shaped him, but that didn't define him.

With that realization, Aryan smiled—a quiet, tentative smile, but it was a smile nonetheless.

He put on his jacket, grabbed his keys, and left the apartment. The city outside felt different. He felt different.

Not healed. Not whole. But free.

CHAPTER THIRTEEN

Moving Forward

The weight of the world seemed a little lighter now. Aryan had spent so long in the dark, trying to navigate the wreckage of his heart. But now, something had shifted within him. It wasn't that the pain was gone—no, the pain was still there, woven into the fabric of his thoughts, a constant companion that would never truly leave. But there was something more now, something brighter. A flicker of hope, small but undeniable, that life could continue, even without Maya by his side.

He had spent months haunted by the ghost of what was and what could have been. His days had blurred into each other—work, silence, more silence. He had tried to escape in everything—books, alcohol, late-night walks that only deepened his sense of loss. But none of it had worked. The only thing that ever felt real was the memory of her. And even that had become distorted over time, like an old photograph, faded at the edges.

But now, as he sat on his balcony one chilly evening, looking out over the city lights, Aryan realized something profound. Moving forward didn't mean forgetting. It didn't mean erasing the past. It meant acknowledging the pain, accepting it, and allowing himself to keep walking, step by step, without the burden of trying to change what had already happened.

The first time he had let go of Maya, it felt like he was abandoning her, like he was dishonoring everything they had built. But now he understood that moving forward wasn't about leaving her behind. It was about integrating her memory into who he was becoming. He could still love her, in his own way, without being paralyzed by the past. He didn't have to forget to move forward.

And that was the hard part. The letting go. The realization that life continued on, even without the person he thought would be by his side forever.

He closed his eyes and took a deep breath. The world felt alive around him, the hum of the city, the cool breeze on his face, the distant sounds of laughter, the occasional honk of a car. Life was happening, and he was a part of it.

He picked up his phone and scrolled through the contacts list. Her name was still there. He hadn't deleted it. Not yet. The temptation to reach out, to hear her voice, to ask how she was—how she was really doing—was still there. It always would be. But now, instead of acting on that impulse, Aryan paused. He didn't feel the panic of losing her. He didn't feel the urgent need to know where she was, what she was doing. He didn't need to cling to her memory to keep himself intact.

He realized then that he was okay.

That was the strangest part. That, after everything—the sleepless nights, the long walks, the tears shed alone—he was okay.

Not completely healed, not whole, but alive. And in that aliveness, he found something he hadn't expected: peace.

Peace that he could move forward. Peace that he could be himself, without the weight of the past. Peace that he could love her, remember her, but not live for her. Not anymore.

And so, one by one, the small actions of moving forward began to fall into place. He started waking up earlier, taking time to read again, to write, to walk. He said yes to invitations. He laughed more. He made plans with Kabir, who had noticed the shift and had started calling him more often. Aryan didn't feel the need to hide anymore. He didn't have to pretend he was fine, but he also didn't have to wallow in sorrow.

There was a certain freedom in letting go, in giving himself permission to live, even when the world felt uncertain. The future felt open, full of possibilities, yet still fragile. He didn't have all the answers. He didn't know what the next chapter held. But for the first time in a long time, he didn't need to. He was learning to let life unfold as it would, with all its messiness and beauty.

There were still moments of deep longing, of missing her so acutely that it hurt to breathe. But now, those moments didn't consume him. They were simply a part of him, woven into the tapestry of his heart. He no longer tried to fight the waves of grief. Instead, he let them wash over him, knowing they would eventually pass. Sometimes, he would close his eyes and allow himself to feel everything—the love, the loss, the regret, the hope—until it felt like too much to bear. And then, just like the waves, the feelings would subside, and he would be left with the stillness.

He had learned, in this quiet aftermath of their love, that moving forward didn't mean running away from the past. It meant allowing himself to hold it gently, without letting it drown him.

One day, he received a message from Maya. It wasn't a long message. It didn't hold any grand promises or declarations. It was simple, direct.

"I hope you're doing okay. I'm sorry for everything."

The words hit him harder than he expected. The finality of them. The quiet sincerity. And for the first time in a long time, Aryan didn't feel the urge to respond with a flood of words, to explain how he had been feeling, to ask for closure. He didn't need closure anymore. He didn't need her to fix what had been broken. What mattered now was that he was beginning to fix himself.

He took a deep breath and typed his reply:

"Thank you. I'm learning to be okay."

And just like that, he sent it. He didn't linger. He didn't dwell on it. The world kept turning. Life kept moving.

That was the true lesson he was learning: that moving forward wasn't about finding closure, or a perfect ending. It was about accepting the imperfections and continuing anyway. It was about trusting that life, in all its unpredictability, would unfold as it was meant to. And that, despite everything, he was still a part of it. He still had a place in this world, even without her by his side.

And that, for the first time in months, felt enough.

Epilogue

Love doesn't always end in together. Some stories are meant to end so that others can begin. Aryan finally understood: getting over someone wasn't forgetting them—it was choosing to live again, even with the memory of them tucked gently into your heart.

And so I did.

Still haven't got over my ex. But it is a work in progress.

As of today, I am married. But a big space in my heart misses her. Wants her to be happy. Wishes to rotate the earth the other way round and go back in time.
I still spend a few nights alone, weeping under the blanket and wish I had done things differently.

No, I do not compare my wife with my ex. I just know that I could have done things better and trust me, there is always only one love in one life.

"Pyaar hota ek baar hai!"

www.ingramcontent.com/pod-product-compliance
Lightning Source LLC
Chambersburg PA
CBHW020517160726
47991CB00007B/2999